MEET THE FRIENDS

Sharla Scannell Whalen

Illustrations by Virginia Kylberg
Spot Illustrations by Helen Kunzi

ABDO & Daughters
Minneapolis

J
WHA

Published by Abdo & Daughters, 4940 Viking Drive, Suite 622, Edina, Minnesota 55435.

Printed in the United States.

Edited by Ken Berg

Library of Congress Cataloging-in-Publication Data

Whalen, Sharla Scannell, 1960—
     Meet The Friends / Sharla Scannell Whalen.
          p. cm. -- (Faithful Friends)
     Summary: Each of four girls knows what it feels like to be different, and as they become friends, they discover something important about themselves and each other.
     ISBN 1-56239-900-4
     [1. Friendship--Fiction. 2. Individuality--Fiction. 3. Self-confi-dence--fiction.] I. Title. II Series.
     PZ7.W5455Me   1997
     [Fic]--dc20   96-32660
                                                                        CIP
                                                                        AC

1398

TABLE OF CONTENTS

CHAPTER
ONE

THE FIRST DAY OF SCHOOL

Ellie's heart fluttered beneath her crisp, burgundy gingham pinafore, but her feet moved slowly down dusty Quarry Road, towards town.

Her grandmother's little red house, where Ellie Perry had lived since her mother died, was only half a mile west of Oakdale. But Ellie wanted to make that half-mile last as long as she could.

She wasn't very old, yet Ellie had had first days at quite a number of schools. Before she and her father, Reverend Perry, moved in with her grandmother, they had changed residences often. The Church Council was always needing Reverend Perry here or there. Starting at new schools never got any easier. But Ellie was afraid that this one was going to be the hardest of all. Grandmother had told her not to expect to see any other African-American children at this school.

Through Tennessee and Kentucky, she had never

been the only black child at school. Of course, Ellie knew that Grandma Perry was very well respected in Oakdale. Her grandfather had been one of the founders of the quarry. And Oakdale was proud of Ellie's father for having gone down to Kentucky for divinity school. But she was still going to be different at her new school.

Ellie was passing the grove of oaks at the edge of town now, but she was still poking along. Suddenly, she heard voices coming up Quarry Road behind her. In a moment, she was passed by two older girls.

"Good morning," they called out to her as they hurried on.

"Hi," returned Ellie, feeling a little better after the friendly greetings.

Ellie realized there were more footfalls coming from behind her—and this person was dawdling, too. Ellie looked back to see a pair of cheeks growing red as a beet under a blue sunbonnet. The girl in the bonnet was playing with one of her brown braids and looked so shy and scared that Ellie forgot that she was nervous herself and stopped to wait.

"Good day to you," said Ellie, using the expression she had heard her dignified father use.

"Hullo," said the little prairie girl, but without the hearty inflection *her* father would have used.

"Is this your first day at school?" Ellie asked as they walked on. "My name is Ellie Perry," she added.

"I'm Hannah Olson," the girl responded, "And today is my first day. Mama has been teaching me at home the last three years. But she and Pa said they can make do without my help on the farm. They said it's time for me to go to school. But I don't want to go. The town girls will make fun of me, because I'm different."

"Why, that was just what I was thinking—about myself, I mean!" exclaimed Ellie. Her heart had stopped beating quite so quickly, and the two girls' feet were now stepping more swiftly down the road.

§

A half-mile from the opposite side of town, on the small bridge spanning one of the many bends in the DuPage River, another heart beat fast and another pair of feet dragged. This girl's blue sailor dress was faded, but freshly washed and ironed. From a distance, one would have guessed from her tangle of red hair and prominent freckles that this little girl was Irish—even before one got close enough to hear the remnants of an Irish brogue.

Margaret Rose Sullivan had been born in a year when yet another potato crop failed in Ireland. People had begun to starve with the first potato famine, and many crossed the ocean to America. Not all had received a warm welcome. "Now, don't you let them be treating you like a second-class citizen, Maggie," her mother had warned her that morning as she set off for school. "You hold up your head and keep your shoulders back. Being Irish is nothing to be ashamed of."

Maggie knew this. In fact, she liked being Irish. But she didn't like the names that some of the boys called her. She didn't like being different.

§

Just a block from school, Ellie and Hannah looked up to see a girl emerge from the largest house in Oakdale. Her long blonde hair fell across the lace on her maroon velvet dress. She adjusted the matching velvet hat on her head and started down the stairs to the street.

"Hullo, Beth," said Hannah.

The blonde girl hurried down to the street with a smile. "How good it is to see you, Hannah!" she replied. "Why did you stop coming in for Sunday School?"

"Well," replied Hannah. "Pa and Mama sorely needed my help at home."

"It didn't have anything to do with those catty girls making fun of you, did it?" asked Beth.

"Well," said Hannah again. "Maybe a little. Town girls don't seem to like farm girls. Except you, Beth. You were good to stand up for me."

Continuing on together, Hannah made the proper introductions between Beth and Ellie.

As the three girls approached the schoolyard they heard the chanting voices of a group of boys. "Shanty Irish! Shanty Irish!" Hannah knew they were teasing someone, and her face turned pale.

At the same moment, Ellie and Beth pushed forward. "Shame on you!" Beth shouted at the boys, yanking a red-haired girl out from the cloud of dust that had been raised. The girl pulled away from Beth, struggling to land a blow on a member of the teasing gang.

Ellie spoke out in a quiet but powerful voice. "My father says we should pity those who don't know that cruelty comes from ignorance and fear. But right now," Ellie finished, clenching her fists, "you've made me so angry, I don't think I can."

At that moment, the school bell rang, and Hannah pushed Ellie to the steps. Beth pulled in the Irish girl. They went in and took four seats together.

"What's your name?" whispered Beth.

"Maggie," her seatmate answered. "And thank you."

"That's all right," said Beth. "We all know what it's like to be different." The three other girls turned to look at Beth in surprise.

"Egad!" jeered a big boy with sandy hair as he walked up the aisle.

"That was meant for me," explained Beth. "The boys found out that my full name is Elizabeth Georgina Annabelle Dunstable. My initials make up the word EGAD. They like to try to provoke me. Maybe because my family is wealthy." Beth's face flushed, as though being rich was something to be ashamed of. "Or maybe it's because my mother is ..."

Hannah hurried to fill the silence left hanging from Beth's unfinished sentence. "Maybe it's because you're so easy to tease?" she giggled. The four new friends all laughed.

Ellie smiled as the teacher brought the class to order. If they were all different—why then, they were all alike!

How good to have found friends on the first day of school, each of the four was thinking. And yet, facing the rest of the class and the world outside the schoolroom, they each continued to feel—different.

CHAPTER TWO

GUARDIAN ANGELS

Walking homeward after the first day of classes, Hannah and Ellie talked about Maggie.

"Her temper is as fiery as her hair," Hannah chuckled.

"I was thinking," said Ellie slowly, "that it might be a good idea for us to reach the schoolyard a little early tomorrow morning."

"You mean, ahead of Maggie!" Hannah said. "I think that would be a very good idea. But surely she and Ben Tarken will reach some kind of truce soon."

"For the time being," said Ellie, "I think it would be a good idea to be guardian angels!"

As agreed, the two girls met outside Ellie's white gate a half an hour early the next morning. Ellie was munching on a muffin, warm from her grandmother's oven. She held one out to Hannah, then turned to give her calico cat, Cleo, a pat good-bye.

"Ummm," sighed Hannah. "Your grandmother is famous for her banana muffins."

"On special occasions," said Ellie, swallowing, "she puts in shavings of chocolate!"

"Are they always banana muffins?" Hannah asked.

"No, she often makes applesauce or oatmeal and brown sugar muffins."

"We'd better walk a little faster," Hannah said, "or Maggie will get to school ahead of us, after all!"

As Ellie and Hannah hiked down Elm Street, they again saw Beth emerging from her house. The three stared at each other for a moment, then Beth began to laugh. "Are you two early for the same reason I'm early?" she asked suspiciously.

"Maggie!" the three of them exclaimed in unison.

As they reached the schoolyard, they could see that they were the first students there. But their teacher, Miss Delia Devine, was sitting on the steep front steps of the school. "You three are early," she called out cheerfully. "I don't suppose it can be for the same reason I'm early?"

"Not Maggie!" exclaimed Beth.

"That's right," said Miss Devine. "Mr. Moore told me about what nearly happened out here yesterday. It's one thing for the boys to tussle amongst themselves, but another thing altogether to have a girl involved. So it occurred to me that I could use a helper in the classroom every morning before school."

Ellie interrupted, "But if Maggie guesses why you are asking her to come to school early, I wouldn't be surprised if she refused."

"I was worried about that myself," Miss Devine frowned. She stood up and shook the navy checked skirts of her dress. She smiled as she continued, "Well, what if I asked *four* girls to come and help? That way she wouldn't feel singled out."

Ellie, Beth, and Hannah exchanged glances. It would mean coming early every day, but working with Miss Devine would be a treat.

By this time, a group of children was buzzing around the schoolyard, and Miss Devine spotted Maggie. "Why don't you ask her—if you're willing to be here early yourselves, that is."

"We are!" they cried, dashing to meet Maggie.

The four walked into school together. Passing a circle of boys, one called out, "Shanty Irish!" Maggie clenched her jaw.

Maggie didn't seem to suspect a thing when the girls told her about Miss Devine's invitation. But she agreed glumly. "I could help her *after* school, too. I won't have anything else to do."

"What do you mean, Maggie?" Ellie asked gently.

"I mean that I won't be going to baseball practice."

"But girls don't play baseball," Beth said, startled.

"That's exactly what Ben and the other boys say. But I don't see why not. My arms and legs work just as well as theirs do. I can run as fast. And I can throw better than the whole rotten lot of them," Maggie said, beginning to seethe.

"Baseball must mean a lot to you," said Ellie in amazement.

"Yes," said Maggie. "It's because of my Uncle Mike, I suppose. He will be pitching for the Chicago White Stockings. He's hoping they will play against the Spiders next season."

"What do you mean, Spiders?" shrieked Hannah.

Beth grinned. "I thought everyone knew about the Cleveland Spiders. They're only the most famous baseball team in the country! They always win!"

"Not when they play against Uncle Mike," smiled Maggie. "Wait till they see his knuckleball! He taught it to me, but of course I can't throw anywhere near as well as he can. Still, I'm as good as any of the boys on the Oakdale School team!"

"I don't see why they couldn't give you a chance," said Hannah. "Why don't we ask Mr. Moore about it? Isn't he the coach?"

"It's no use," Maggie frowned, "the boys won't have me. Ben made that clear yesterday." Her face looked like a thundercloud.

Beth thought it was time to change the subject. "Can you all come over to my house after school? I want to show you my new riding suit."

The rest of the day passed uneventfully and the four girls headed for Beth's house after school. Crunching apples, they climbed the stairs to Beth's beautiful bedroom.

Hannah had seen the room before, but Ellie and Maggie were speechless. Everything in that room was pink—the wallpaper with its roses on vines, the bedspread and canopy, the curtains, the rug. The dresser and armoire were painted pink. Even the wastebasket was pink!

"Somebody sure likes pink," said Maggie with some distaste. It makes me feel as though I've eaten too much pink cotton candy."

Beth turned away from the mirror, which stood on a pink vanity table, where she had been retying a ribbon in her long, golden hair. "Well," said Beth, "I do like pink. But the room was really my father's idea. When I was a baby, he used to say I was 'pretty as a pink.' A pink is a kind of flower, you know. He started calling me 'Pink,' and he still does, sometimes."

"I think it's sweet," said Ellie. "Both the room and the story."

"It's sweet all right," groaned Maggie.

Beth laughed and squeezed Maggie's arm. "I really like you, Maggie. If you ever give me a compliment, I'll know that you truly mean it—because you obviously say what you think!"

Maggie continued to inspect the room as though she were slightly sick to her stomach. "It's too bad dogs don't come in pink," she said, grimacing at the fluffy white dog sitting on a pink footstool.

"I like Snowflake the way he is!" said Beth, picking him up for a hug.

Hannah was admiring the beautiful fabric of the bedspread. "Where did you ever find such cloth?" she asked.

"My father ordered the curtains and bedspread from New York City," Beth said.

"Your father?" Maggie asked. "Wouldn't your mother be more likely to do it?" Suddenly, she remembered Beth's unfinished sentence about being made fun of because of her mother.

"Beth's mother lives in Paris," Hannah explained.

"So, my parents don't live together," added Beth. "And that is something that people in this town like to talk about. They like even better to whisper about the fact that my mother sings in the Paris Opera. They seem to think that my father and I should be very ashamed of that." Beth looked as though she *were* rather ashamed.

"I would love to meet your mother," Hannah said.

"My mother would love to hear your lovely singing voice, Hannah," smiled Beth. "I was so disappointed when you didn't sing for the Sunday School program last spring."

"I just didn't feel comfortable in town," said Hannah. "But I have the feeling that this year is going to be different! Now, where is that riding outfit? Did it come from New York, too?"

"No," said Beth. "It just came out on yesterday's train from Chicago." Beth pulled a large box marked "Marshall Field's" from a hand-painted pink chest. "I haven't even opened it yet. I wonder what Papa will have sent for my birthday. It's only sixty-eight days away."

"Sixty-eight days?" exclaimed Ellie.

"Well, yes," answered Beth. "I like to start counting down the days early."

"I should say you do!" giggled Hannah.

Beth began untying the cording around her box while Maggie looked lost in thought. "How much does it cost to take the train to Chicago?"

"Twenty-five cents each way," Beth said. "I take the train to Sommerfield every week for my riding lesson. That's less than half way to Chicago, so it costs ten cents. Are you planning a trip to Chicago, Maggie?"

"Yes. I want to go to West Side Park in two weeks," Maggie said. "My Uncle Mike will be playing. The White Stockings don't give him a chance to play very often because he just started with them. But he'll be playing in the exhibition ballgame. He said so last week. He comes out to see us every Sunday."

"So that's how you learned to play baseball," Hannah said.

Maggie nodded. "My brother Kevin will take the train in with me. He has money for his ticket, but not for mine, too. Now how am I going to earn the money for the train fare?" she asked herself out loud.

"Maybe we can all help think of something," said Ellie.

Beth opened her box and pulled out a beautiful riding suit. The riding pants were a rich, chestnut brown, and the jacket was a tan and chocolate-colored plaid.

"It's beautiful," Ellie breathed.

"At least it's not pink," Maggie grumbled.

§

CHAPTER THREE

NO GIRLS ALLOWED

A cross the river was a large vacant lot, bordered by a wooden fence on two sides. Maggie visited this lot every day after school. She kept her treasured baseball glove stored under an old tin pail behind a thicket of forsythia bushes by the first house on that side of the river. She had used charcoal to draw a large bullseye on the fence. Pacing the distance to an imaginary pitcher's mound, Maggie fired off pitches at the bullseye. The woman in the nearby house was quite deaf, so no one seemed to notice Maggie's practice sessions. That is, until one day an errand brought Mr. Moore, the school's baseball coach, to the east side of town.

He heard the rhythmic bang of the ball hitting the bullseye as he walked along the other side of the fence. At the end of the lot, he looked around the boards and was surprised to see a sweaty-faced Maggie winding up for another pitch.

Bang! The ball hit the center of the bullseye.

"Whew!" said Mr. Moore aloud. "You've got quite an arm there! Where did you learn to pitch like that?"

"From my Uncle Mike," Maggie replied. "Michael Sullivan. He plays for the White Stockings."

"With an arm like yours," Mr. Moore said, "you'll be playing for the White Stockings yourself one of these days."

"Girls don't play baseball," said Maggie bitterly. "At least, that's what the boys at school say—especially Ben."

"Hmmm," mused Mr. Moore, rubbing his chin. "We'll see about that. There's a practice after school tomorrow. Can you be there?"

"Yes," Maggie responded slowly, "but ..."

"Just be there!" said Mr. Moore.

The next day was hot, with a dry wind coming in from the wide prairies, blowing the dust on the crude baseball field behind the school. The team was already practicing when Maggie returned from the vacant lot with her leather glove.

"What are you doing here?" snarled Ben.

"I asked her to stop by," said Mr. Moore.

"Girls can't play baseball," said Ben. The other boys muttered assent.

"I could strike you out, Ben Tarken," Maggie said angrily.

"I'd like to see you do it," Ben challenged.

"Let's give her a try," said Mr. Moore. The boys looked at him in surprise.

"Aww, let her go back and play with her dolls," taunted Ben.

Daniel O'Leary looked at Maggie thoughtfully. "What's the matter Ben—afraid she'll strike you out?"

"She's only a girl!" said Ben. "Okay—this won't take long. Try it, shanty Irish."

As Maggie slowly walked to the pitcher's mound, her anger seemed to fade. Standing there, glove on her left hand, she seemed to be in complete control of herself—and of the situation.

Ben took up the bat. Maggie wound up and fired her first pitch—straight past Ben's head. Ben dove for the ground. As he got up and began slapping the dust from his clothes, he looked at Maggie with a white face. "You did that on purpose," he said, his mouth pinched with anger.

Maggie shrugged calmly. "Wanted to see how your reflexes were. Now let's see if you can bat."

"That was ball one," said Daniel.

The next pitch whistled across, leaving Ben swinging at thin air. Then Maggie threw two that missed the plate.

Ben barely got his bat on the next pitch, fouling off the ball.

"Strike two," Daniel called out.

"Here comes the last pitch, Ben," said Maggie with that strange calmness which had come over her. "And how about this—if I strike you out, you promise never to call me 'shanty Irish' again!"

"He shouldn't call you that, or any other name," said Mr. Moore. "I suggest that if Maggie can strike out Ben, we make her part of our team."

Ben and the other boys nodded their agreement. Maggie wound up her last pitch. It went straight for the plate, and it looked as though Ben couldn't miss—until the ball wobbled to the side just before plunking into the catcher's mitt.

"A knuckleball," whispered Mr. Moore.

"Strike three!" Daniel shouted, and a great cheer went up. Ben stood silent as the boys rushed to the pitcher's mound to slap Maggie on the back, as though she were one of them.

"This is going to shed a whole new light on the Westbrook game!" said Daniel. "Maybe Maggie will even throw a no-hitter!" Maggie beamed, and Mr. Moore looked very pleased. Ben stood, grim-faced.

CHAPTER FOUR

MUFFINS FOR SALE

As she pushed open her grandmother's white gate before the stroll to school, Ellie exclaimed to Hannah, "I've got it!"

"Got what?" asked Hannah, taking the ginger muffin which Ellie held out to her.

"Muffins!" exclaimed Ellie, holding hers up. "We can sell muffins to help Maggie earn her train fare."

"What a wonderful idea!" said Hannah admiringly. "I love it! Do you think your grandmother would help us with the baking?"

"I've already asked her," said Ellie, "and she thinks it will be very educational for us! Not only will we learn about muffin-making, but she thinks we should set this up as a real business with a partnership of four."

As the girls helped Miss Devine in the classroom before school, they talked it over. They would use their first profits to reimburse Ellie's grandmother for the supplies they would need for the first batch. After that, they would set aside a portion of their earnings to pay for the mixings for the next batch, dividing the remaining profit equally. Miss Devine chuckled about their serious attitude and said that she thought their big plans sounded exciting.

"It's a good thing tomorrow is Saturday!" said Hannah.

Eager to get started, the foursome met at Ellie's house first thing the next morning.

"I don't usually get up this early on Saturday," Beth yawned. "But I can't wait to smell those muffins baking!"

They had decided to make banana muffins for their first endeavor in the baking business. Beth insisted that they leave out nuts. "I can't abide crunching into a nut in a nice soft muffin."

"All right," said Mrs. Perry. "But what do you say to a piece of walnut right on the top, just for decoration?" She set Maggie to slicing up the shelled walnuts while Ellie beat eggs and Hannah and Beth crushed bananas.

In no time, the Perry kitchen was filled with the rich aroma of banana muffins rising from the wood-burning stove. After the muffins were cool, the girls loaded them into two baskets lined gaily with checked cloths. They covered the cakes carefully and set out towards town.

They stopped at a big blue house with gingerbread trimming around the porch. The woman who answered

the door smiled at the four expectant faces. Two boys
and a little girl clung to her skirts. She bought three
muffins. Hannah put the coins into a small purse.

"Hannah's our treasurer," laughed Beth. "It was good
thinking to bring along that purse."

"And now we've got our first profits!" said Ellie.

"Not yet," reminded Maggie. "First we have to pay
your grandmother back for the eggs and flour and
everything."

"Grandmother said she wanted to contribute the
fixings for our first batch," said Ellie.

"I don't think we should let her do that, though," said Hannah. "Since we're a real business, we've got to act businesslike!"

Before the girls had gone far along Elm Street, all their muffins had been sold. They stopped at Beth's house where Hannah calculated their earnings. She reported that they would have enough to pay back Ellie's grandmother, plus buy ingredients for another four dozen muffins.

"Great!" exclaimed Beth. "Next week, let's put chocolate shavings in."

"No, we won't have enough money by then," Hannah insisted. "We probably will the week after that. But we'll have to charge more for the muffins, since it will cost more to make them with chocolate."

"This really is a business!" said Ellie.

The next week, the girls earned enough money for ingredients—even chocolate—for the following week, plus a ten-cent profit apiece.

"At this rate," said Maggie, "I'll have enough for the train fare in time! And my mother suggested an idea. She thought we should add scones to our inventory. She'll give us her best recipes."

"Our business is expanding!" said Beth with satisfaction.

CHAPTER FIVE

ALL ABOARD!

At last the big day arrived when Maggie and Kevin were to take the train to Chicago. That morning, the girls met to make their baked goods at the Dunstables'. Beth's house was closer to their customers and they wanted to get done early. Beth was just finishing her bowl of Shredded Wheat when the other girls skipped in.

Agnes, the family cook, had Saturday mornings off, so the girls had the kitchen to themselves for their scone-making. They were surprised when Beth's Aunt Mary popped into the kitchen and actually spoke.

"You might sprinkle some basil or oregano into that mixture," she said stonily. "It will make them more palatable."

"Thank you, Aunt Mary," Beth responded cheerfully. "Is palatable your 'word for today'?"

"No, today's word is 'ubiquitous,'" Aunt Mary said, stalking back out of the kitchen, her gray skirts swishing starchily.

"I know you wouldn't think it from the stiff way she acts," Beth whispered to the others. "But she's really a dear."

"Well," said Maggie, "I think a little basil sounds like a good idea—though, to tell the truth, I'm not sure what it even tastes like."

"It's used in Italian cooking, I think," said Beth. "But I think it would be interesting to try it in scones!"

"But what did you mean by her 'word for the day'?" asked Ellie.

"Since she was a child, Aunt Mary has made it a goal to learn a new word every day," answered Beth.

"She must know an awful lot of words!" Ellie exclaimed, looking as though she liked Aunt Mary's idea.

Hannah was rummaging among the many tins in the spice cupboard. "How does Agnes keep track of all these spices and extracts?"

"She doesn't," said Beth. "She's always misplacing the rosemary or the vanilla or something."

"Here's the basil," said Hannah. "Ummm, it smells good!" Hannah passed the basil to Maggie as she set about putting the tins in alphabetical order. "Let's see, allspice, almond extract, ..."

Soon the savory-smelling scones were taken off the

cooling racks, the pretty baskets were loaded, and the girls were out on Elm Street.

Mrs. Martin-Mitchell, who lived in Pine Craig, a large brick mansion, had made Beth promise to stop there first. "I'm having a tea this afternoon," Mrs. Martin-Mitchell explained. When she smelled the scones, she rolled her eyes and sighed. "Heavenly," she exclaimed. And she bought their entire inventory!

"Well," said Maggie, as they walked away with their empty baskets. "We'll have no trouble making the train on time, Beth!"

The girls returned to Beth's house until it was time to go to the depot. Beth and Aunt Mary always took the 10:45 train to Sommerfield for Beth's riding lesson. Maggie and Kevin planned to take the same train, which continued to Chicago.

Hannah and Ellie tagged along to see the travelers off at the beautiful train station. On the outside, the walls were half-timbered, like an old English house. Inside, there was a vaulted ceiling and gleaming oak walls and floors.

Kevin had been able to get most of the day off from the mill, but he had had to work until 10:30. He came dashing up to the platform, just a few minutes before the train arrived.

"Got the tickets, Maggie?" he called out breathlessly.

"Right here," she said, waving the yellow slips of paper.

"And I've got the refreshments!" he said, holding up a white paper bag. "I stopped at McGuire's and got a dime's worth of candy." With a grin, he offered a stick of Juicy Fruit to Aunt Mary. Surprisingly, she accepted it.

With a roar and a rush, the locomotive puffed into the station and they all got aboard. "My word," said Hannah, looking around at the shining woodwork and the green plush seats. She'd never been on a train before. "It's beautiful."

The group said their good-byes, and Hannah and Ellie returned to the platform and waved until the train was out of sight.

The journey was extra special for Maggie, since she was riding with both Kevin and Beth, not to mention Aunt Mary. As they rode, sitting together, Beth told them about Chicago. "My most exciting trip into the city was for the World's Fair, three years ago. I was pretty little, but I could never forget my ride on the giant wheel. I met George Ferris, too. He built the wheel, and he's a friend of my father. That wheel could hold over two thousand people at the same time, and each car on it was bigger than this train coach."

"I didn't go to the Exposition," said Maggie, "but I remember the first day of it. That was the first time we said the 'Pledge of Allegiance' at school. We were living in Boston then. It was just after we'd come over from Ireland."

"That's right," said Beth. "My father knows Francis J. Bellamy, too. He wrote the 'Pledge of Allegiance,' and he's the editor of the *Youth Companion*."

"I love the stories in that magazine," said Maggie. "Your father certainly seems to know a lot of important people."

Beth nodded. "He's hoping that will help him in politics. He's running for the Town Council in November, you know. But about Mr. Bellamy—he wanted children across the country to have a chance to participate in the dedication of the fair. So he wrote the 'Pledge of Allegiance' to the flag. It was sent out to all the teachers in the country. And millions of children all said the Pledge for the first time on Columbus Day in 1892. It was exciting to think of so many children saying the same words, all at the same time."

"And here it is," Maggie said, "four years later and lots of children still say the 'Pledge of Allegiance' every morning at school. I wonder how long it will last? I hope we keep it up while I'm in school—I like it."

As it turned out, the ball game was canceled half way through, due to a drenching downpour. But Maggie had seen her uncle pitch, which was what she'd wanted to make the trip for, after all.

On the train ride home, Maggie thought about everything her new friends had done to help her dream come true. "I'll pay them back somehow," she whispered to herself.

CHAPTER SIX

HANNAH'S SECRET

Hannah was unusually quiet as she and Ellie walked home along Quarry Road after leaving the train station.

"Wish you were taking a trip, Hannah?" Ellie asked.

"That's right," Hannah said. "Trains seem so romantic to me. I want to ride those rails myself! But it was a treat just to see the inside of one of the cars."

Hannah waved goodbye with a smile as Ellie turned in at the white gate. She hadn't told Ellie the whole truth. Of course, trains *were* romantic and she *did* wish she could ride them. But it was what trains symbolized to her that had made Hannah so quiet and thoughtful on the walk home. The wail of the train whistle always made Hannah think of the world beyond Oakdale. She didn't want to settle down on a neighboring farm, as her married sister Rachel had done. She wanted to go out into the world that the train rails led to, out into Chicago and beyond. What she wanted to do was to sing. But the only person she knew who had done that was Beth's mother. And no one wanted to talk to her about Beth's mother. Was there something shameful about a singing career? Of course, most women didn't have careers at all. But Hannah thought that there was no reason why a woman who wanted a career shouldn't have one.

The next Monday, Hannah was still somber. As she and Ellie walked to school, she was as quiet as she had been on Saturday.

"All right," said Ellie. "What's bothering you. Are you still hankering after a train ride?"

"No, it's not that," said Hannah. "But I don't think my parents will be happy about it, so I shouldn't talk about it."

"Sounds pretty serious," said Ellie wonderingly.

"I want to sing," said Hannah solemnly.

Ellie burst out laughing. "I'm sorry," she said. "It's just that I was expecting you to confess something shocking!"

"Maybe this is shocking," said Hannah. "I want to sing in big concert halls and maybe in an opera. I'm not sure exactly. But I don't want to grow up and get married right away, like Rachel. I want to grow up and sing."

"Well, why don't you?" Ellie asked.

"Because I have to have lessons, and lessons cost money," said Hannah. "We just can't afford it."

"What are you going to do with your baking money?" asked Ellie.

"That's only enough for a lesson or two. And now that we're done baking, there'll be no more money."

"Why do we have to be done baking?" demanded Ellie. "I don't see why we can't keep it up every Saturday. We may have started to help Maggie with a way to earn money for train fare. But that doesn't mean it has to end there."

"I suppose not," said Hannah in her slow, deliberate way.

As the four girls worked in the empty classroom that morning, they talked it all over, again with Miss Devine as a sympathetic listener.

"Mrs. McGuire used to sing in concerts," encouraged Miss Devine.

"She did?" exclaimed Hannah. "I can't believe it!"

"I think she'd be happy to take you as a pupil. Would you like me to ask her about it?"

"Yes, thank you, Miss Devine. Just as soon as I've talked to my parents about it."

"Of course, dear," said Miss Devine approvingly, as she reached for the school bell.

The girls had decided to go out to the Olson farm with Hannah after school. It was the first time they had come to her home, and Hannah was somewhat self-conscious. But she was the only one who seemed to think of the differences between town girls and farm girls. And she was also grateful for their moral support. Hannah dreaded trying to explain to her parents how she felt about singing.

Hannah was surprised by her parents' reaction when she told them.

"It's about time we had another singer in the family," her father said. "Haven't heard any trills since Rachel was in high school." They also approved of the girls' intention to continue their baking business.

"But the business is going to need a name," said Mrs. Olson. "What will it be?"

"How about 'Best Bakers'?" suggested Ellie.

"You 'Best Bakers' come out here next Saturday morning to do your baking," said Mrs. Olson. "And I'll have a little surprise for you," she added mysteriously.

The following Saturday, the girls gathered in the Olson kitchen. Hannah's smiling mother brought out four gingham aprons, each checked in a different color and each embroidered with the words "Best Bakers." Mrs. Olson handed the green one to Ellie, the blue to Maggie, yellow to Hannah, and pink to Beth.

The girls thanked Mrs. Olson as they tied on the aprons. Maggie looked at Beth primping in her pink gingham apron, tied over a pink sailor suit. "How did you ever know?" she asked Hannah's mother.

Hannah, observing the three "town girls" moving busily about her kitchen, chatting happily with her mother, suddenly realized that she didn't feel different anymore!

CHAPTER
SEVEN

BASEBALL & BUTTERFLIES

Another week of mild autumn weather passed quickly by. Maggie had settled in at school, and the girls no longer felt the need to get there early in order to prevent an altercation between Maggie and Ben. The two weren't friendly, but there were no longer any loud squabbles. So Maggie's temper seemed to be fading, along with her freckles. But they knew it would be flaring up again—just as her freckles would be reappearing when the summer sun came back.

Nevertheless, the girls found themselves continuing to come early to school. They enjoyed helping Miss Devine in the classroom, and Miss Devine relished hearing about their adventures and their plans.

"You know," Miss Devine said to them one Friday morning. "I've never done it before, but I believe I'm going to come out to that baseball game tomorrow afternoon, Maggie. Henry—I mean Mr. Moore—is always encouraging the faculty to support the team." To

40

the girls' mystification, Miss Devine blushed.
"Besides," she said, straightening the already very
proper white collar of her blouse, "you girls have been
talking about the game so much, I'm downright curious
to see how it comes out. Does Westbrook really have
such a fine team?"

"They haven't lost all season," Maggie replied.

"Neither have we—thanks to you and your pitching
arm, Maggie," Hannah interjected.

"It's only three games," Maggie said modestly. "And
we have a field full of good players."

"Are you nervous, Maggie?" Ellie asked.

"Heck, no," Maggie answered. But Ellie noticed that
Maggie's face was stormy.

"This will be a special game," Miss Devine said,
"since it will be the debut of your custom-made
uniform."

"That's right!" Maggie shouted, the sun coming out
on her face. "Mother finished it yesterday! And I want
to thank you girls again for advancing me your baking
profits."

Hannah, Ellie, and Beth had insisted that Maggie
borrow their shares from the Saturday baking in order
to buy the fabric for certain adjustments to Maggie's
team uniform. Maggie could pay it back, they offered,
over the rest of the autumn.

Mr. Beebe at the dry goods store had to special-order the creamy white cloth with its thin red stripes. Maggie's mother was a swift seamstress and had made the necessary changes. The trouble was, though the school board had made no objections to a female addition to the baseball team, they insisted that she be dressed "modestly." Girls could not be seen wearing pants. Maggie thought this was as ridiculous as the idea that girls couldn't play sports.

Miss Devine sympathized. "There are times," she said, "when these long skirts are a real nuisance—it's impossible to run in them." Miss Devine rustled her stiff, ankle-length maroon skirt.

"Fortunately," Maggie added, "the skirt on my baseball uniform is only to my knees. And mother made it very full, so I'll be able to run!" Maggie would be permitted to wear the knicker-length trousers of the uniform under her skirt, so that she could slide. "Only two more days until the game," Maggie said.

"Only thirty-two more days until my birthday," Beth sighed. They all looked at her and laughed.

Once again, the girls got an early start with their baking on Saturday morning. They had finished up in plenty of time for Maggie to meet the team at school for the drive to Westbrook. Daniel O'Leary's father drove a large group in his farm wagon, including Maggie.

As the horses drew them closer and closer to Westbrook, Maggie's anxiety increased. She wished Kevin could be at the game, but he couldn't get away from work. She wished the game was being played on the Oakdale field. And she wished the butterflies would stop fluttering in her stomach. She also thought that she would feel more comfortable if there wasn't a player called "the Slammer" on the other team.

It was a lovely October afternoon. Maggie saw the crisp, blue sky and the canopy of red and gold leaves overhead. She knew it was beautiful, but she couldn't seem to feel it. And she heard the voices of her teammates, but she couldn't seem to understand what they were saying.

In a fog, she found herself on the field. The game was starting. The Oakdale team was up first. The boys struck out with only one run to show.

Then it was time. Time for Maggie to go out to the mound. She walked the first batter. The next two hit singles. Now the bases were loaded. Then the Slammer, a clean-up hitter, came to the box. Maggie tried to summon her courage, but she mostly shivered.

Her pitching arm was numb. And the Slammer lived up to his name. He hit a grand slam on her first pitch, bringing in four runs. He'd cleaned up, all right.

"A girl pitcher!" the Slammer sneered, as he crossed home plate. Things went from bad to worse, as Maggie allowed eight more runs before the inning ended.

"It's all right, Maggie," said Mr. Moore, patting her on the back.

"No, Mr. Moore," Maggie said firmly. "I don't want you to go through another inning like that. I'll be sitting out the rest of the game."

Mr. Moore could tell by her tone that Maggie meant what she said. He snatched a glimpse of Miss Devine sitting in the rough, wooden stand. Miss Devine put a finger to her lips. Mr. Moore understood that she thought he ought to let Maggie have some time to sort things out. He just said, "Okay, Maggie."

At the top of the next inning, Daniel took over the pitching. He did well (though he glanced at Maggie mournfully, from time to time), and by the end of the eighth inning, Westbrook was ahead by only one run.

Meanwhile, Maggie had been sitting dazed and glum. At last she glanced at her friends. Beth was glaring angrily toward the Slammer. Hannah's face was rigid, and Ellie seemed fretful. Maggie looked at Miss

Devine, who was looking at her. Miss Devine met Maggie's eyes and smiled warmly. Maggie felt the numbness begin to drain away. She began to think. After all, the worst had happened. She had choked. It couldn't get any worse. Nothing to be afraid of now!

Maggie then heard a cry from the field. The Westbrook batter had hit a line drive, striking Daniel squarely in the right shoulder. Mr. Moore ran out to inspect.

"Nothing broken," said Mr. Moore, walking Daniel to the plank bench. "But," he said, looking at Maggie, "he won't be doing any throwing for a week or two."

"I can do it, Mr. Moore," said Maggie, jumping to her feet and picking up her glove. She didn't feel cold anymore. Her arm felt positively hot. She grinned at Daniel. "You're one heck of a pitcher, Dan," she said.

"But I'll never throw a knuckleball that can flutter like yours!" Daniel answered.

This time Maggie struck out the first two batters with the Oakdale fans cheering. When the Slammer stepped up to bat again, Maggie looked him straight in the eye.

"Who ever heard of a girl playing baseball?" he jeered. "Why don't you go home and play with your dolls?"

Before Maggie could reply to the taunt, she heard a voice from the Oakdale bench. It was Ben.

"Maggie," he shouted. "Give 'em the pitch!"

Maggie looked over at Ben. She narrowed her eyes and smiled. Ben grinned back, and Maggie nodded. She struck out the Slammer with knuckleballs, three in a row. The Oakdale fans roared approval. With more cheers coming from the bench as well as the sidelines, Maggie realized that she didn't feel "different" any more. She belonged—to the team as well as to her friends and to Oakdale.

On the way home in Mr. O'Leary's wagon, Ben muttered, "You know, I guess girls *can* play baseball." But when he glanced over at Maggie, his face was still sour.

"He's one tough nut to crack," Maggie thought to herself.

§

CHAPTER EIGHT

THE SPELLING BEE

On their way to school one chilly morning early in November, Ellie said to Hannah, "Ben expects to win the spelling bee." For the first time, there was a dusting of frost across the empty corn fields on either side of the road.

"Well," said Hannah, "I expect he will win. I heard him say that he's won the spelling bee three years running."

"Maybe his winning streak is over," Ellie said mysteriously.

"Maybe," answered Hannah. "So do you think we ought to bake cherry muffins tomorrow?"

Hannah didn't know that Ben was going to have competition this year in the spelling bee. Ellie knew.

The spelling contest was held that afternoon. Miss Devine asked the class to come to their feet. The students lined the walls of the room. Their class, being the largest in the school, also had the biggest room.

Standing shoulder to shoulder around the four walls, they just barely fit. But before long, there was more elbow room, since Miss Devine began with words from the "Difficult" list.

"I thought she was going to start with the 'Easy' list," Maggie whispered to Beth.

Back in September, Miss Devine had given the class three word lists. They were marked "Easy," "Difficult," and "Impossible." Maggie had never gotten beyond studying the "Difficult" list. She thought she was a pretty good speller and hoped that there would be a winner before Miss Devine progressed too far through the "Difficult" list. But competition for the spelling bee was fierce. There were quite a few students who had been hoping to beat Ben and had taken the word lists very seriously.

Maggie was surprised by the number of students still standing after the first pass around the room. She herself had hesitated over "chrysalis," but had remembered the "h" in time. Beth had gone down on "eland." Hannah and Ellie were still up. So was Daniel O'Leary. But Daniel went down in the second round. So did Hannah and Maggie. By the third round, those left standing covered only two walls. By the fourth round, only one wall of students was left. Ellie was still up. Maggie, Hannah, and Beth looked at each other—and at Ellie—in

wonder. They hadn't known that Ellie was a great speller. "I wonder what other hidden talents she has?" Maggie whispered to the others.

Before long, there were only three spellers left: Ben Tarken, Murgatroyd Forsythe, and Ellie.

"Murgatroyd has been studying his brains off," Daniel said to Maggie. "He's bound and determined to beat Ben."

"Maybe he will," said Beth.

"Maybe," Hannah contributed, remembering her conversation with Ellie before school that day. "But I think Ellie is going to do the 'Impossible.'"

All three had managed to spell the first three words on the "Impossible" list. But Murgatroyd stumbled on "aardvark." And on the very next word, Miss Devine shook her head at Ben after he had incorrectly spelled out "Quetzalcoatal." All eyes watched Ben return to his seat, and Miss Devine said, "Ellie?"

Ellie cleared her throat. "Quetzalcoatal. Q-U-E-T-Z-A-L-C-O. . ." she hesitated, then added confidently, "A-T-A-L. Quetzalcoatal."

"She did it!" Daniel exclaimed. "She beat Ben! Three wins and he's out!"

The class applauded Ellie's victory enthusiastically, and she smiled back, shyly. She looked around at all the happy faces and realized that she didn't feel different anymore—in fact, she hadn't for some time!

Miss Devine presented her with the first prize, a pocket-sized dictionary. "Will you write in it, Miss Devine?" Ellie asked.

Miss Devine wrote on the inside of the cover, "Congratulations to Ellie, our champion speller, who is full of surprises."

Outside, after school, the four friends stood talking. After Beth reminded them that her birthday was now only six days away, they had begun planning their choices for the next day's baking. They were surprised when Ben approached.

"Congratulations, Ellie," he said, extending his hand.

"Gee, Ben," said Maggie, " No one could say you're a sore loser."

"I guess I figure," returned Ben, "that if you can't beat 'em, join 'em." They all laughed.

When Ben turned to look at Maggie, there was no sourness to his smile.

CHAPTER NINE

BIRTHDAY SURPRISES

Maggie exclaimed, "Do you know, I'm going to be relieved when Beth's birthday is finally over—so we won't have to hear how many days away it is."

"That's not true," objected Beth. "Why, the day after my birthday, my birthday will be 364 days away!"

Hannah, Ellie, and Maggie groaned while Miss Devine, writing a lesson on the blackboard, began to laugh.

"You're not serious," said Hannah. "You don't really count down the days until your birthday all year long?"

"Okay, I'll wait until there are fewer than a hundred days to go," promised Beth.

"Beth," said Miss Devine fondly, "you are a character."

"As long as that's a compliment!" sang out Beth as the girls started for the door.

The Town Council election was held that week and Beth's father was among the winners. Beth was pleased, but she was even more excited that her birthday was the next day. "How do you think my father will try to surprise me?" she asked her friends for the hundredth time.

"I know, I know," said Maggie. "You always manage to guess the surprise beforehand."

"But I haven't guessed it this year—that is, not yet!" Beth admitted.

When Beth returned home after school, she went directly to her bedroom. She sat at her writing desk, which was the only piece of furniture in the room not painted pink! It was of gleaming cherry wood. The flat writing surface was hinged, so that it could be folded up to close the desk. Inside were several cubby holes and two small drawers. It was an antique, sent from her mother in Paris. Her mother had told her that the desk had belonged to a courtier at the time of Louis the Sixteenth, right before the time of the revolution. That was over a hundred years ago. The desk held the romance of the court secrets it might have overheard. And it reminded Beth of her mother.

Beth opened one of the drawers and removed a sheet of white stationery with a border of pink roses. She began a note to her mother. She always started her letters the same way: "Dear Mother, I hope you are well, as we are all here at present." It sounded very formal and made quite a contrast to the rest of her letter, which was an outpouring of all that Beth was doing and feeling.

Beth loved writing to her mother and receiving letters in return. But it was sometimes unsatisfying, as she knew that it would be many weeks before her mother would read the words she wrote today. She realized that her birthday would be long past by the time her mother received this letter, but it still felt good to share her anticipation.

"Usually, I have some idea of Daddy's surprise. But this year, I haven't a clue," she wrote. Beth leaned her hand on her chin and twirled her yellow hair around an index finger. She finished the letter and folded it up. She drew a stick of pink sealing wax from her stationery drawer. The metal seal had her initials entwined with flowers and vines. She would have to go down to the kitchen to light the wick.

Nearly the entire city of Chicago had been destroyed by a terrible fire in 1871, and Aunt Mary had made her promise never to light a match without help from an adult. But Beth wasn't finished decorating her envelope. The sealing wax would come last.

Beth's father had given her a miniature metal printing press as a birthday gift years ago. She had produced a household newspaper for a while, but it hadn't lasted long. She ran out of news. Perhaps she and her three friends could think of a way to use the printing press sometime.

The set included small printing plates with drawings of flowers, pretty ladies, and animals. Beth selected a tiny plate with roses and inked the drawing from a bottle with a spongy tip. She had inks in several colors. And her father had been sure to include pink! She used pink on the roses and imprinted the image several times around the edge of the envelope. "There!" she said, as she blew the ink dry. "Almost done."

She skipped down the narrow back stairs to the kitchen, carrying the letter in one hand and the pink wax and seal in the other. As she went whistling into the kitchen, she was startled by a commotion. Agnes and Gertie, the downstairs maid, were hustling out the other door in a whirl of white—something. It looked like feathers. Agnes came back in the room with a smile and tears welling in her eyes.

"Are you needing help with your wax, dear?" she asked Beth, wiping her eyes on her apron.

"What's going on, Agnes?" Beth demanded.

"It was just the cook from next door, come to tell us a funny story about the butler up at Pine Craig. Now, let's have your wax."

Beth put the seal into the hot melted wax on the flap of the envelope and thanked Agnes. Turning to go back up to her room, she noticed a long, fluffy white feather lying on the floor.

§

Miss Devine's classroom was buzzing with stifled excitement the next day. Beth knew that the whole class had been invited to her party. That aspect of her birthday was predictable. Her father was a great believer in including everyone. "We wouldn't want to have any hurt feelings," he would say.

And she knew that her party would be at the supper hour. So she was puzzled after school by the inactivity in Agnes' kitchen. She had expected to find sauces bubbling and pleasant odors coming from the stove. But Agnes was just watering the bright red geraniums on the wide windowsill above the sink. The whole house was quiet, but Beth was too stubborn to ask any more questions. So she went up to her room to change clothes and wait for her father to come home.

Beth's birthday dress had been sent out on the train yesterday. She opened the large gift box with excitement. Inside was a white eyelet dress with a low waist, trimmed with pale pink ribbon. There was a little purse to match, white eyelet with a pink drawstring. Inside was a pink hankie, a small ivory comb and a tiny bottle of cologne water. The label said it was from Paris.

Aunt Mary appeared to help Beth with the pink hair ribbon which had come with the dress. Aunt Mary drew it across the top of Beth's blonde head and tied it at the back, under her hair. The ribbon was dotted across the top with pink rosebuds.

Dressed for the party, Beth sat on the bed petting Snowflake morosely. "I'm mystified," she said to herself. "And I don't think I like it a bit." This was the first year when she was really going to be surprised. Her father came in shortly, smiling broadly.

"Hello, Miss Pink," he said, trying not to laugh at the look on her face. "Ready to go?"

"Go where?" asked Beth suspiciously.

"Why, to your party, of course," her father said innocently. "Let's move!"

They walked down the wide front steps, carpeted in an oriental design of blue and red. Mr. Dunstable helped Beth with her blue velvet cloak and led the way across the large open hall, out the front door, and down the stairs. His carriage, drawn by a pair of white horses, was waiting in the street.

"Where are we going?" cried Beth. "Where is Aunt Mary? Where is everyone?"

"You'll see," her father smiled. "Have I finally surprised you?"

"Yes," Beth said somewhat glumly. "You have."

"Why, Beth," Mr. Dunstable teased, "I thought you liked surprises!"

"I guess what I liked was figuring out the surprises, and this time I couldn't. Unless it has something to do with feathers."

"Feathers?!"

The carriage soon drew up in front of the train station. "What are we doing here?" Beth asked.

"You'll see," her father said again.

The spacious station had been transformed into a fairy land, with yards of white tulle draped in loops across the ceiling and fresh greenery twisted up the columns across the waiting room. In the center of a huge table, also draped in white tulle, sat an enormous cake with two tiers. It was iced in pink with white roses. And all around the table stood her classmates. They cheered as she came in. Aunt Mary was there too, and Agnes.

"What is this all about? This is the strangest birthday party I have ever seen."

"Come over and see your cake, Beth dear," said Miss Devine. Miss Devine pointed to the top of the cake, and Beth leaned over it to read the words, "Welcome Home!"

"Welcome Home?" Beth said, her eyebrows high in mystification. At that moment, a loud dissonant whistle sounded from the door leading to the tracks.

"There's no train at this time of day," Beth exclaimed.

"No, no train," said her father. "But there is an arrival."

The doors were suddenly pushed open and, in a swirl of white feathers, in walked—Beth's mother!

"Mother!" shouted Beth, catapulting into her arms, dodging the white feathers on her mother's boa.

The children cheered louder than ever at the happy reunion. Miss Devine settled them down by announcing that it was time to serve the cake. Beth and her mother cut the first piece. Hannah, Maggie, and Ellie came to be introduced to Mrs. Dunstable, then the four girls settled into a window seat to eat their portions. They were joined by Ben and Daniel and several other classmates.

"Well, I guess you were finally surprised," said Ben.

"No more trying to guess birthday surprises for me," said Beth.

Hannah, watching Beth's mother and father chatting by the cake table, asked quietly, "Has your mother come home to stay, Beth?"

"No, I know better than that," Beth said. "And I know better than to expect her to live with my father anymore. She doesn't belong here. She's part of a different world, in Paris. But I also know that she loves me, so it's all right. And though she doesn't belong here, I know that I do."

Contemplating the room of smiling faces and disappearing cake, Beth realized that she didn't feel different anymore.

"Wait a minute," she said, looking thoughtful. "There was no train. Where did that whistle come from?"

"I don't know," Maggie answered. "Let's go ask."

Beth's mother took her daughter by one hand and beckoned to the other girls to follow.

Outside the doors, sitting on a railing eating cake, were two high school boys. Beside each sat a cornet.

"Beth would like to hear the train come in again," said Beth's mother in her deep voice. "You take 'E' this time, and you take 'D'," she ordered the two boys.

The boys got up and blew the two notes. Together, the dissonant chord sounded exactly like a train whistle. They all laughed, and the boys returned to the rail to finish their cake.

"When did you come in, mother?" asked Beth.

"On the morning train. And when I stopped by to see

Agnes, I think you almost caught me. But it's cold out here—let's go back in!"

The chill November wind blew the feathers from Mrs. Dunstable's white hat as she turned to the door with Beth, Maggie, Hannah, and Ellie.

"Feathers!" Beth's eyes widened as one white feather fluttered to her feet.

The transformed waiting area still looked like a train station in fairy land. Mr. Dunstable was waiting beside the cake table. He held four small boxes, two in each hand. Mr. Dunstable smiled as Beth approached him expectantly.

"Four?" she asked.

"Four," he said. "One for each."

The other girls giggled. "But it's not our birthdays, Mr. Dunstable," Hannah protested.

"I know," he said. "But this four-way friendship has meant so much to Beth this fall, I wanted to take a moment today to celebrate it." He presented each girl with a little box, dripping with narrow satin ribbon. "You'll find a friendship ring inside, with the stone of your birth month."

Inside Beth's box was a pinkish-yellow topaz; in Maggie's an amethyst with its purple glow; in Hannah's a tiny emerald; and in Ellie's a small ruby.

"You'll also find a gold necklace in each box," Mr. Dunstable went on, "to wear the ring on, for the time being. I selected rings which are a little too large—for you to grow into. In a few years, you can wear them on your fingers. You see, I know this special friendship between the four of you is going to last and grow with you, too."

"I have a feeling that you're right, Father," Beth agreed. The four friends thanked Mr. Dunstable. Then linking arms, they dashed off to join their classmates.